Princess Ponies

The Lucky Horseshoe

The Princess Ponies series

Princess Ponies

The Lucky Horseshoe

CHLOE RYDER

BLOOMSBURY
CHILDREN'S BOOKS
NEW YORK   LONDON   OXFORD   NEW DELHI   SYDNEY

BLOOMSBURY CHILDREN'S BOOKS
Bloomsbury Publishing Inc., part of Bloomsbury Publishing Plc
1385 Broadway, New York, NY 10018

BLOOMSBURY, BLOOMSBURY CHILDREN'S BOOKS, and the Diana logo are
trademarks of Bloomsbury Publishing Plc

First published in the United States of America in January 2019
by Bloomsbury Children's Books

Text copyright © 2017 by Awesome Media and Entertainment Ltd
Illustrations copyright © 2017 by Jennifer Miles

Bloomsbury books may be purchased for business or promotional use. For information on
bulk purchases please contact Macmillan Corporate and Premium Sales Department at
specialmarkets@macmillan.com

Library of Congress Cataloging-in-Publication Data
available upon request
ISBN 978-1-5476-0164-6 (paperback) • ISBN 978-1-5476-0165-3 (e-book)

Printed and bound in China by Leo Paper Products, Heshan, Guangdong
2 4 6 8 10 9 7 5 3

All papers used by Bloomsbury Publishing Plc are natural, recyclable products
made from wood grown in well-managed forests. The manufacturing processes
conform to the environmental regulations of the country of origin.

To find out more about our authors and books visit www.bloomsbury.com
and sign up for our newsletters.

With special thanks to Julie Sykes

For Cody

The Pony

Queen
Moonshine

Princess
Crystal

Princess
Cloud

Princess
Stardust

Princess
Honey

Royal Family

King
Firestar

Prince
Jet

Prince
Comet

Prince
Storm

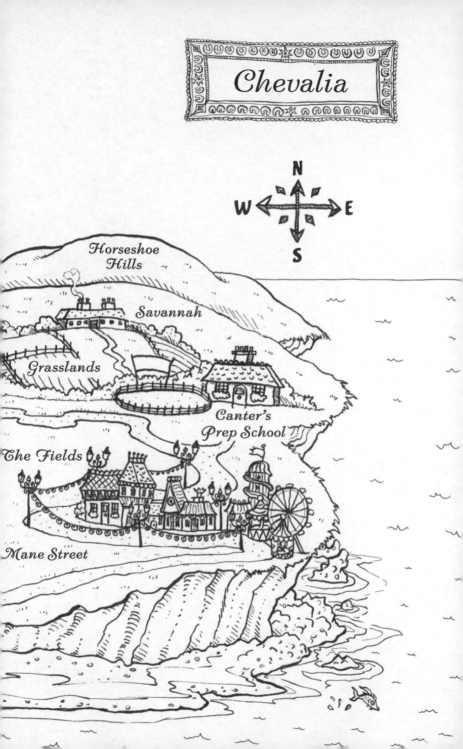

Far away, in the middle of the sea, there's a magical island called Chevalia, where only ponics live. Chevalia is a special place, full of love and happiness. It's ruled by the wise Queen Moonshine and King Firestar from the Royal Court at Stableside Castle.

But a long way from Stableside, in the middle of the Horseshoe Hills, there was a smaller, crumbling castle with ivy-covered walls. Mice and beetles scurried through the empty rooms. Bats roosted in the towers and spiders hung from thick webs.

In a dingy room at the back of the castle, a chestnut pony with bulging eyes and a square nose was watching a band of metal glow in the fire. Green flames crackled up the chimney as the metal twisted into a horseshoe shape. Taking a long pair of tongs, the pony, whose name was Divine, removed the horseshoe from the flames and dropped it into a bucket of cold water. The water hissed and spat. Dark green clouds of steam rose from the bucket as Divine removed the horseshoe and carefully dried it on a scrap of an old horse blanket.

"It's ready!" Divine felt the horse-shoe strain, pulling what little luck was in the room toward it.

The dark-green horseshoe twitched and jerked, then at last it stilled. Divine shrugged on a cloak and pulled up the hood to cover her smile. She popped the horseshoe into her satchel.

"Ponies of Chevalia, your lives are

charmed. But not for long! The unlucky horseshoe is ready. With it, I shall steal all the luck from Chevalia." Divine gave a loud cackle. "Bad luck, ponies. The spell has started. When fortune fails Chevalia, I will claim my place as its rightful ruler."

Chapter 1

It was March 17, lucky St. Patrick's Day, but Pippa MacDonald was not having a good day.

At breakfast, Pippa's older sister, Miranda, had finished off her favorite cereal, leaving only the dust at the bottom of the cereal box.

"Bad luck," Miranda had said. "The early bird gets the worm."

Pippa didn't want to eat worms, just

a bowl of her favorite Clover Corn cereal. Instead, she had to make do with Mom's boring oatmeal.

Then, in a rush to get to school, she tripped on the front steps in front of everyone. The older kids laughed at her, and Miranda said, "Get up, clumsy."

Later, Pippa hurried to change into her gym clothes. But because she was ready first, her teacher Ms. Tilley asked her to run back to the classroom to fetch the whistle she'd forgotten. When Pippa returned with the whistle, gym class had started and her friends were already assigned to groups.

"You're in teams of four today," Ms. Tilley told Pippa. "Join in with Lucy's group."

"But I always work with Cody," said Pippa, smiling as Cody waved her over.

"Cody's team is full. Hurry along. Lucy's waiting for you."

"It's not fair," muttered Pippa.

Lucy hated gym class and so did her

friends Sasha and Peter. They spent most of the time messing around, making it impossible for Pippa to focus on the exercises. Today the class was practicing climbing the ropes. Pippa didn't like heights, though she tried her best.

"Look at me," called Peter, swinging from his rope. "I'm a monkey."

"You look like a monkey," Lucy said with a laugh. She and Sasha started making monkey noises.

Peter kept bumping into Pippa, making it difficult for her to climb to the top of her rope. At the end of the lesson, Ms. Tilley called the group over.

"I'm disappointed in you four," she

said. "You can stay behind and pack the equipment away in the storage room."

"That's so unfair," whispered Cody. She hung back to help Pippa, but Ms. Tilley sent her back to the classroom.

"This is just not my lucky day!" groaned Pippa.

The afternoon was just as bad. In art class, her favorite green glitter pen ran out before she'd finished her St. Patrick's Day picture. Then Cody accidently knocked a jar of dirty painting water over, ruining the picture completely.

"I'm sorry!" wailed Cody. "Here, have my picture instead."

"That's okay." It was kind of Cody, but she hadn't meant to spoil Pippa's work. It was just bad luck.

"Today can't get any worse," Pippa grumbled out loud as she walked home from school, her umbrella up to stop her from getting wet in a sudden heavy downpour. She thought longingly of sunny Chevalia and her best pony friend, Stardust. If only she were there now. That would be a lucky day!

Whoosh—Splat!

A car sped through a muddy puddle, spraying Pippa from head to toe.

"Bad luck, Pippa," said Miranda. "Lucky for me, I didn't get splashed."

When they got home, Pippa started heading upstairs to change out of her muddy school clothes, but her mom stopped her. "There's a special surprise in the kitchen. Go and say 'hello.'"

Pippa trailed after Miranda. She wasn't in the mood for surprises. The way her day was going, she'd be lucky if it was a good one!

A friendly-looking lady was at the table sipping a cup of tea.

"Aunt Maeve!" Miranda ran across the kitchen and hugged her aunt.

"Pippa and Miranda, my favorite nieces." Aunt Maeve laughed and put her cup down. Her black hair was tied in a ponytail and her green eyes sparkled. "Well, that's two nice hugs, one from Miranda and one from Jack. What about you, Pippa? Do you have a hug for your auntie?"

"Hi, Aunt Maeve." Pippa sidestepped her little brother, who was sitting on the floor playing with a toy leprechaun. She wrapped her arms around her aunt and hugged her tightly. "It's so good to see you."

"To be sure. Only, your face is telling me a different story. What's up, Pips?"

"Not much." Pippa sighed. "Things keep going wrong. Bad luck is following me around today."

"Luck's a funny thing," said Aunt Maeve wisely. "Sometimes you have it; sometimes you make it; but once in a while your luck runs out, and there's nothing you can do about it. Today I'm feeling *very* lucky. I'm spending St. Patrick's Day with my sister and my wonderful nieces and nephew. But I remember a time when I didn't feel so lucky. I was the same age as you, Pips, and living in a tiny village in County Galway."

Pippa's aunt Maeve was from Ireland and only visited every few years. But Pippa always loved her stories of what Mom called "the old country."

"Now, County Galway is a beautiful part of Ireland," Aunt Maeve continued, "just the right place for having a pony. We even had a big field next to the house to keep one in. But there wasn't enough money for luxuries, so I had to make do with Shanks's pony. That's Irish for 'my feet!' One day there was a huge storm that ended with a beautiful rainbow. Everyone in Ireland knows there's a pot at the end of the rainbow full of leprechauns' gold. I was determined to find that rainbow's end and buy myself a pony. I put on my boots and set out. I walked for miles, getting stuck in mud, falling over in a puddle, making holes in my boots, but I never caught up with that rainbow."

Aunt Maeve sighed. "It was a bad-luck day, for sure. I was about to turn around, when I spotted a ruined cottage. In the field next door, there was a pony. I couldn't believe it! She was a golden

Connemara, and you could tell that she'd been beautiful once. Not anymore, though. She looked like she was starving, poor thing! Her bones stuck out and she needed a good grooming. Her golden fur was thick with mud, her mane and tail tangled, and her brown eyes full of sadness."

"Poor pony!" Pippa sighed, remembering her summer vacation and the well-kept, shiny-coated, bright-eyed ponies she'd ridden at the riding school. "What did you do?"

"The pony needed food and, as I didn't have any on me, I started to pull up the grass in the lane. The pony was chomping it down when a girl about the same age as me came along. No

Shanks's pony for her. She had a brand-new bicycle. It was super fancy, with a basket and everything. She told me that the pony was hers and she was fed up looking after it. She offered to swap it for my lucky necklace, a gold coin on a chain. I told her that the necklace hadn't brought me any luck, but she said it was prettier than the pony and a lot less hassle. So I gave her the necklace, she gave me the pony, we shook on the deal, and then she cycled away."

"And you took the pony home," breathed Pippa.

"I couldn't!" exclaimed Aunt Maeve. "I didn't have anything to lead it with. I ran all the way home to fetch a rope and something for the pony to eat. It took me ages and when I got back, the field was empty. My new pony had gone!"

"No! Are you sure you went back to the right place?"

"Definitely! There was no mistaking that ruined cottage. I checked the field and it had hoofprints in it. There had been a pony but it had mysteriously vanished. I never saw the girl again either." Aunt Maeve sniffed away a tear. "When I told my parents, Ma said it was good to have such a wonderful imagination, but I didn't have to tell stories to explain why I'd lost my necklace. Da said the same."

"That's so sad!" Pippa understood how Aunt Maeve must have felt. Adults never believed her either, especially when she told them about Chevalia, the magical island where her talking pony friends lived. "That story makes me feel lucky!"

Aunt Maeve nodded. "Whenever I feel that my luck's run out, I remember my poor underfed pony. I think about all the good things to eat in my pantry; my friends and family, especially my wonderful nieces and nephew; and suddenly I'm the luckiest person in Ireland."

Pippa smiled at her aunt. She had lots of things to feel lucky about too!

Much later on, after a riotous sing-along with Aunt Maeve playing on the bodhran, an Irish drum, Pippa lay in bed wondering about the starving Connemara pony. What had happened to her? Ponies didn't just disappear! Pippa closed her eyes but as she drifted off to sleep, a sharp whinny made her sit up straight. She sat in the dark listening and then she heard it again. A high-pitched whinny followed by the rattle of stones on glass.

Pippa ran to the window. She flung back the curtain and, pushing the window wide, she gasped at the sight before her.

It was a crew of pirate ponies!

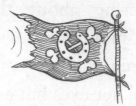

Chapter 2

"Ahoy there, Pippa MacDonald," a familiar voice boomed up at her.

Four ponies had gathered on the lawn under the window, and Pippa recognized their leader.

"Captain Rascal!" Pippa carefully leaned out to look at him. Captain Rascal was a sturdy black-and-white horse with a neatly cropped mane, wearing a three-cornered pirate's hat and a purple eye patch. "What are you doing here?"

"We've come to take you back to Chevalia."

"Is there trouble again? Do you need help?"

"Aye, you could say that. Hurry up, there's no time to lose."

"On my way." Pippa drew back inside and silently threw on some clothes. The landing outside her bedroom was in darkness. She could hear loud snores from Jack's and her mother's bedrooms. On tiptoe, Pippa crept downstairs, past the pull-out sofa where Aunt Maeve was sleeping, and let herself out through the back door. There was no need to leave a note. Pippa had been on many adventures in Chevalia and knew that no time passed in her own world when she went there.

Outside, a thin moon lit the garden. Pippa ran across the wet grass to Captain Rascal and his ragtag crew.

"Up you hop," said Captain Rascal.

Pippa eyed him doubtfully. He was a lot taller than Princess Stardust, her best princess pony friend. Luckily, Captain Rascal was near a flowerpot. By standing on it, Pippa was able to climb on his back.

"Anchors up and make sail!" called Captain Rascal.

Pippa grabbed at a handful of mane as Captain Rascal trotted through the garden and into the street. He had a rolling gait that reminded Pippa of a boat sailing on the sea. The pirate ponies trotted through the sleeping neighborhood. Pippa hoped they wouldn't wake the neighbors and was relieved when they arrived at the park at the end of the street. Pippa guessed they were heading for the river, but her breath caught in surprise when she saw the enormous boat tied up on the bank.

Purple and gold sails hung limply from the three wooden masts. A smaller, triangular black flag drooped from the top of the tallest. Even in the dark, Pippa could clearly see the white horseshoe and crossbones pictured on it. Cannons lined the boat deck. Pippa's stomach flipped with excitement.

"*The Jolly Horseshoe*," she whispered, reading the pirate ship's name from the bow.

A blue-and-red parrot perched on the ship's wheel watched her with interest. "Pieces of eight, Pippa's late," he squawked.

"Permission to come aboard," said Pippa, smartly saluting.

"Permission granted." Wearing a pink tiara, a pretty white pony with a long white mane and tail stepped out of the shadows.

"Princess Stardust!" Pippa slid from the captain's back, raced across the hoof plank, and threw her arms around Stardust's neck.

"I knew you'd come." Stardust softly blew in Pippa's wavy brown hair. "Chevalia needs your help again."

"Stand by to set sail," boomed Captain Rascal.

The pirate ponies began to sing, out of tune but with lots of enthusiasm.

Lift the hoof plank, one, two, three.
Away we sail on the deep blue sea.
A pirate's life is the one for me.
A pirate's life on the bluey blue sea.

Pippa pushed her hair away from her face. "Where in Chevalia are we going first?" she shouted against the sudden burst of wind.

"To find a pot of gold," said Stardust. "To pay Divine to stop using the unlucky horseshoe to steal all of Chevalia's luck."

Pippa's face creased with puzzlement. "How can a horseshoe be *unlucky*?"

"Divine put a spell on it. The

horseshoe acted like a magnet. It attracted all the luck in Chevalia to it."

"It's a bad business," said Captain Rascal. "Nothing's gone right since Divine stole all the luck. We lost a sail when a rope broke and we almost ran aground earlier today. Divine's keeping the luck for herself until we pay a hefty ransom in gold. Luckily, my grand-mother, the great pirate pony Captain Scallywag, hid a pot of gold somewhere on Chevalia's coast. And we're going to find it!"

Pippa was surprised. It wasn't like Divine to simply want money. Divine wanted respect, and she wanted to rule. "Are you sure this isn't another plan to rule Chevalia?" she asked.

"I don't know," said Stardust. "But I do know this. My big sister Princess Crystal broke her tiara this morning and you know how careful she is! And remember my friend Blossom? She was training for the next Equestriathon when she tripped and sprained a hoof. Queen Moonshine's in complete despair. She doesn't approve of ransoms, but without luck, Chevalia is doomed."

"That's awful!" said Pippa, but at the same time she couldn't help feeling a little thrilled. Another adventure in Chevalia! "Where are we going first?"

"We're going to search the caves and coves of Chevalia to locate that ole treasure," Captain Rascal chimed in. "We'd like you to join us, Pippa

MacDonald, lover of ponies; you are our good-luck charm!"

Pippa didn't want to be anyone's charm, but she was happy to help since the ponies were in trouble. "I'll do my best," she said. "But I'm not feeling very lucky."

The wind picked up as *The Jolly Horseshoe* left the shelter of the estuary for the open sea. Pippa clutched the handrail and peered into the night. Stardust was speaking. Pippa could see her mouth moving but the howling wind caught her words and tossed them away. The boat dipped and rose. Pippa stood with her feet wide to stop herself from falling over on the pitching deck. Soon, the waves were taller than Stable-side Castle. The wind tossed the spray at the ship, drenching Pippa in cold water. Stardust nudged Pippa's arm and nodded at the cabin.

"Good idea," gasped Pippa, the wind snatching her breath away.

Slowly, clutching each other, Pippa and Stardust fought their way across the open deck.

Stardust opened the cabin door and started to go belowdecks, but Pippa stopped her.

"We won't be able to see when we reach Chevalia. We should stay up here, in case we miss something."

"Good point," said Stardust.

They huddled together in the doorway, but they couldn't escape from the wind and spray.

"It's freezing," Stardust said with a

shiver, her teeth chattering. "Please, can we go inside?"

The boat jumped and bucked like a wild horse. Pippa's heart leaped with it. Were they going to capsize? Captain Rascal must have thought so too for he ordered the pirate-pony crew to take down the mainsail.

"Whoaaa!" Stardust clung to Pippa as the boat tipped suddenly.

Pippa hung on to the door with both hands to stop herself from sliding across the deck and into the churning water. If the pirate ponies didn't get the mainsail down quickly, they were going to capsize!

"The sail is stuck," said Stardust.

The purple and gold sail was

stretched like an overfull balloon. No matter how hard the pirate ponies pulled on the rope, it wouldn't budge. Squinting her eyes against the spray, Pippa stared at the mast. The rope was caught on a wooden cleat.

The boat lurched again. The sea rushed closer. For a split second, time seemed to stand still, with the boiling water beneath them and the wind roaring above. With a shudder, the boat righted itself, smacking down and creating a spray of water to match the thunderous waves.

There was only one thing to do. Someone had to climb the mast and free the rope before the ship capsized or sank.

Me, thought Pippa, knowing she was the most agile. She took a deep breath as she gathered up all her courage. *Forget how high the mast is*, she told herself as she sprinted across the deck. *Look up. Never down.*

You can do this.

Chapter 3

As Pippa climbed the mast, Stardust called out, "Pippa, be careful!"

Pippa nodded but didn't dare look back at Stardust. She focused on her hands as she pulled herself up the mast. The boat pitched and rolled on the sea, as if it was trying to shake Pippa off. She climbed higher even though her clothes were soaked and her hands so cold it was hard to get a grip on the mast. Water dripped from her wavy hair and she could taste salt on her lips.

"I can do this!" Pippa said as she took one tentative step at a time, until at last she reached the hook-like cleat. The wet rope was wound tightly around it and stretched taut by the billowing sail. Pippa's fingers were frozen and clumsy.

Gritting her teeth, she struggled with the rope, loosening it from the cleat with her fingernails. Just when she thought she couldn't untie it, the rope came free.

"Yay!" Pippa's heart soared as the mainsail collapsed, flopping onto the deck like a stranded jellyfish.

"Hooray!" came the call from below. Stardust's cheer was the loudest of the bunch. Without looking, Pippa gave her friend the thumbs-up.

Climbing back to the deck was much easier with the mainsail down. The waves were still huge and the wind wild, but the boat felt more stable. Pippa reached the deck and collapsed, panting as she got her breath back.

"What luck you were here. We

couldn't have done that without you," said Captain Rascal, clapping Pippa on the back. "Pirates, take her downstairs. Give her a blanket and a cup of hot chocolate."

"Wait!" cried Pippa as Stardust started to hustle down the cabin stairs. "What's that, to the left of the boat?"

"Left!" screeched the parrot. "Left is for landlubbers. Pippa's a landlubber."

"What's that, to the *port?*" Pippa corrected herself.

A short way from the boat, two heads bobbed in the water, watching Pippa with big eyes.

"Triton and Rosella!" Pippa felt a tingle of magic pass through her as Triton, the green seahorse, and Rosella, the pink one, swam toward *The Jolly Horseshoe*.

"Hello, Pippa, lover of ponies," said Rosella, softly. "We hear you've come to return the luck to Chevalia."

"With Stardust and the pirate ponies," said Pippa, her face turning as pink as Rosella's skin.

"So modest," said Triton in his sing-song voice. "Throw us a line and we'll tow you out of this storm."

"Really? Thanks!" Pippa looked to Captain Rascal, who pointed with a hoof to the rope Pippa needed. She threw it overboard and Rosella caught it in her mouth. Triton swam to help her and together they towed the boat to a place where the sea was calm and the sky bright blue.

"Thank you!" called Pippa.

"You're welcome. Our magic is too strong for Divine; she couldn't steal our luck, so we're giving it to you."

Pippa felt another tingle, like a soft breeze.

"Use our luck wisely, Pippa." Triton

and Rosella dipped their heads and, with a flick of their delicate ears, swam away.

The tingling feeling grew stronger, then gradually it faded. Pippa smiled. She felt so lucky and full of hope. Triton and Rosella were magic! With their help, she could restore the luck to Chevalia.

"Land ahoy!" shouted Captain Rascal.

"Chevalia!" Stardust and Pippa cheered, rushing to the deck rail, their eyes pinned to the shore, searching for gold and the unlucky horseshoe.

"That's too tiny to be Chevalia," said Captain Rascal. "Fetch me my telescope, Pirate Hoofpick."

"Aye, aye, sir." A tiny chestnut pony

saluted smartly and trotted below-decks. Minutes later, he came back with a telescope.

Something in the corner of Pippa's eye caught her attention. She turned her head and stared at the now flat sea. What had made it ripple like that?

Captain Rascal peered through his telescope. "Well, I never," he muttered. "I don't remember that island being there."

There was a loud bang and the boat juddered. Stardust's brown eyes widened as she gripped Pippa. "What was that?"

"Cow sharks!" roared Captain Rascal. "Well, I'll be a parrot's papa! Cow sharks are attacking the bow. Stand by to repel these scurvy attackers."

"Cow sharks!" Stardust's white coat turned even whiter.

Pippa ran to the bow and blinked in surprise. Four cow sharks were circling in the water. She hung over the side, fascinated by these strange creatures. The cow sharks each had a triangular fin that stuck out of the water. Their bodies were gray-blue and resembled a shark, but their tails were long and cowlike with a fluffy tip, which they used to swat at the seaflies circling above the water around them. The cow sharks had the head of a cow, big with velvety ears, large eyes, and soft black noses. Their mouths were more frightening, shark-like with rows of huge teeth that glinted in the sunshine.

The cow sharks swam in an orderly group, taking turns to bite the bow of the boat. Each time one took a mouthful, the boat swerved erratically.

"Help!" squeaked Stardust. "We're going to be eaten alive."

Captain Rascal strode down the deck. "Prepare to fire the cannons!" he ordered.

The pirate ponies swung into action. Running to the lockers at the rear of the boat, they pulled out a stash of heavy iron cannonballs.

"Form a chain!" called a pirate with a gold ring in one ear.

"Don't be a pain, form a chain," echoed the parrot.

The pirate ponies formed a long line that stretched from the lockers all the way along the deck to the cannons. Deftly they passed the cannonballs along the pony line, where the end pony, a tall black horse with one wooden leg, popped them into the cannons.

"Take aim!" the captain ordered. "Prepare to fire, and . . ."

Pippa had been staring into the water. Something about the cow sharks bothered her. What were they doing? Pippa had studied sharks last year in science class and recalled that when sharks attacked, they formed a circle around their victim, who was usually in the water. She'd not heard of them attacking a boat before, at least not a big boat like *The Jolly Horseshoe*.

"Wait!" Pippa cried. "Hold your fire."

Chapter 4

"Excuse me!" Captain Rascal almost fell over in surprise. "Who's the captain around here?"

"You, of course." Pippa reddened. "But the cow sharks aren't attacking us. They look like they've got something stuck in their teeth."

"Stuck in their teeth, that's Pippa's belief," chirped the parrot in a disbelieving voice.

"They do!" said Stardust. In her excitement she leaned too far over the edge of the boat. Pippa grabbed hold of her and pulled her back before she toppled overboard.

"Thanks, Pippa. It's seaweed!" Stardust added breathlessly. "They're using the ship's bow like a giant toothpick to remove the seaweed from their teeth."

"They'll never get the seaweed out like that!" Pippa stared around the boat thoughtfully. She'd once gotten a piece of apple stuck between her teeth, and it had been very irritating until Mom had given her a strand of dental floss to remove it. What could they use to help the cow sharks? The closest thing to dental floss was rope, but that was too thick, even for the enormous teeth of the cow sharks. As Pippa's eyes traveled the boat, they came to rest on a lifeboat, suspended above the deck. Her face broke into a smile.

Pippa ran to the lifeboat and took out a wooden oar. She carried it to the ship's bow, calling "Come and help me!" to Stardust as she passed.

"What are you going to do?"

"Watch," said Pippa, "and hold on to me, so that I don't fall overboard."

Stardust wrapped her hooves round Pippa's middle as she leaned over the side of the boat.

"Hello, cow sharks," Pippa called out. "Line up and I'll help you to clean your teeth."

The cow sharks' eyes widened in surprise.

"It's a girl!"

"That's not just *any* girl, Velvet," whispered the smallest cow shark. "That's Pippa MacDonald!"

"You're right, Daisy!" replied Velvet, who had two small horns. "I've always wanted to meet her. Aren't we lucky that she's out here on the open seas!"

Obediently, the cow sharks formed a line with Daisy in front.

"Open wide and say 'ah,'" said Pippa, repeating what the dentist told her on her last visit. Carefully, she angled the oar into the waiting cow shark's mouth and scraped out the seaweed trapped between her teeth.

"Oooh, that feels better," mooed Daisy. The cow shark ran her long, rubbery tongue over her teeth. "Thank you, Pippa."

"Thank you, Pippa," chorused the other cow sharks after Pippa had cleaned their teeth.

"This is our lucky day," said Velvet.

"We were *very* lucky to swim into Pippa MacDonald."

"Thank you," said Pippa. "It's a lucky day for me too. I've always wanted to meet a cow shark."

Stardust threw her a puzzled look.

"I would have if I'd known they existed," Pippa whispered.

Velvet continued. "Have you come to hear the music?"

"Music?" Captain Rascal's ears swiveled with interest. "What music? We love a good sing-along, don't we, pirate crew?"

"Aye, aye!" roared the ponies.

"Then you must visit Hoofishbofin, the island to your west. The ponies there make the best music around," said

Daisy. "We often swim by to listen to them sing."

"Hoofishbofin? Never heard of it," said Captain Rascal. "Come to think of it, I didn't know that the islands around Chevalia were inhabited by ponies. But much as we love to sing, we haven't got time today. We're off to find pirate gold."

"Then you must definitely visit Hoofishbofin," said Velvet. All the cow sharks nodded in agreement. "Rumor has it, there's gold on the island."

"Why didn't you say that earlier? Thanks, cow sharks. Full steam ahead, pirate crew, to the island of Hoofish-bofin."

Pippa couldn't help worrying as they

waved good-bye to the cow sharks.
What if the rumors of gold were just
that, rumors? They'd be better off
looking for the unlucky horseshoe.

"We won't stay long," said Stardust,
guessing her concern. "And if there
isn't any gold, then the pirate ponies
will work better for having a sing-
along."

The Jolly Horseshoe creaked and
juddered alongside the small wooden
jetty on Hoofishbofin Island.

"All ashore, me hearties," called
Captain Rascal when the hoof plank
was lowered.

Pippa's wavy hair blew around her
face as she followed Stardust ashore.
She held it back with a hand as she made

for the shelter of a rocky outcrop. Stardust joined her and they huddled
together while they waited for the
pirate ponies to disembark.

"Listen," said Pippa. "I can hear
music."

It was impossible to stay still. Pippa
temporarily forgot about the unlucky

horseshoe as she headed toward the music, her feet dancing in time with the merry tune.

"That music sounds just like the kind my aunt Maeve's band plays." Pippa hummed along, sometimes making up words to the tunes.

As Pippa turned a corner, she stopped, clapping her hands in surprise. "An outdoor theater!"

Tiers of seats were carved into the rocky ground around a raised circular stage, where four ponies were singing. Two were also playing fiddles, while one played a harp that was almost as tall as Pippa; and the fourth pony, a pretty golden Connemara, was keeping the beat with a small drum.

"That's a bodhran!" Pippa clapped her hands in delight. "Aunt Maeve plays one."

As they approached the stage, the song finished. The musicians bowed to each other. They laid their instruments down and the gold-colored pony shared out a pile of coin-shaped tokens. The

ponies lined up to take turns at flicking the coins into a round, black pot.

"Tiddledyhooves!" cried Stardust. "I love tiddledyhooves. Can I play?" she called, trotting on ahead.

The ponies turned in surprise.

"Visitors!" The golden pony had a musical lilt to her voice. "Now there's a rare thing, to be sure. And who might you be?"

Stardust stopped in surprise. "Don't you know?" Her chest swelled with pride. "I'm Princess Stardust, royal foal of Queen Moonshine and King Fire-star."

"Well, I'll be clovered! Welcome to our humble island of Hoofishbofin." The pony dropped a curtsy. "I'm Connie and these are my band members: Rowan on the harp, Kira and Alby on fiddles. Our band's known as the Happy Hooves."

Stardust curtsied back. "Nice to meet you. Now, please can I play tiddledyhooves?"

"To be sure." Connie tossed a token at Stardust. It glittered as it spun through the air. "Your friend can play too, if she likes. It's a long time since I've seen a real girl!"

"Wait!" Pippa caught the token aimed at Stardust. She held it out in the flat of her hand. "Look!" she breathed. "It's not a tiddledyhoof. It's a gold coin."

"Shiver me horse bones!" Captain Rascal trotted over to the black pot. "I thought I recognized this pot. It belonged to my granny, the great Captain Scallywag. The cow sharks were right. There is gold on the island. Great Captain Scallywag's pot of gold."

Chapter 5

Connie threw back her head and laughed. "You'll be telling me that this old thing is your granny's horseshoe next!" She pointed her hoof at an ancient horseshoe on the ground. "Anyone want a throw? Whoever gets it the farthest wins the game."

Stardust wrinkled her nose. "Eew! I'm not touching that."

Something stirred in Pippa's mind.

"Can I see?" she asked, holding out her hand for the horseshoe.

Connie passed it to her. Pippa's heart thumped with excitement as she examined the green-tinted shoe.

"Careful," said Captain Rascal. "Hold it with the two ends pointing upward or else the luck will run out."

"Thanks." Pippa righted the horseshoe and handed it back to Connie. "I thought it might be the unlucky horseshoe," she explained. "But it feels quite normal. The green stuff is moss, not magic."

"But the pot of gold did belong to my granny," Captain Rascal insisted. "I can prove it. Her initials are engraved on the bottom." He tipped the pot over. "There, *CS*. Captain Scallywag."

"Please, can we have it back?" Stardust gave Connie a winning smile.

Connie almost fell over, laughing. "Whatever for? Don't you have everything you need at the royal castle?"

"It's not for me." Stardust's ears turned pink. She quickly explained how they needed to find the unlucky horseshoe to return Chevalia's stolen luck and find the gold to pay Divine, to stop her from stealing their luck again.

When she'd finished, Connie let out a relieved sigh. "You don't need gold to keep your luck. You need attitude!"

"What do you mean?"

"Let me tell you a story." Connie beckoned for everyone to come closer.

Pippa, Stardust, and the pirate ponies shuffled forward, eager to hear Connie's tale. Pippa was squashed between Captain Rascal and Stardust, but Connie had started and she didn't dare move for fear of missing anything.

"A long time ago, when I was a youngster, I came from a faraway place inhabited by humans and where ponies were kept as pets."

A gasp rippled among the pirate ponies.

Connie nodded. "It's true. Many of those humans were good people." She smiled at Pippa, who flushed. "Sadly, my human was young and selfish. It wasn't long before she tired of me. Her visits became less frequent. Often she forgot to feed me, and she never brushed me or cleaned my hooves. But I never stopped hoping that one day my luck would change and I'd find a better life. And one day my luck did change. There was a storm that ended in a rainbow. Shortly after the rainbow appeared, a kind-looking girl with long black hair came to my field. She was shocked at how thin and dirty I was. When my human arrived on a shiny new bike, she asked to swap me for the kind girl's lucky-gold-coin necklace. It was obvious that the necklace was special to this girl, but my owner took the necklace and cycled away. It was the last time I ever saw her. The kind girl patted me and promised that she'd give me food and shelter. Then she went away."

Connie's eyes misted at the memory. "I didn't have to wait long. Soon after, a beautiful silver, winged pony flew over my field. She hovered in front of me as she told me all about Chevalia, a magical place where every horse had plenty to eat and a warm stable to sleep in. She said she'd come to take me there, and she rubbed her nose against mine. *Poof!* In a puff of glittery gold smoke, suddenly, I had wings too. I flew away with the pony."

Connie paused. "We were nearing Chevalia when we flew over Hoofishbofin. Someone was playing music and it seemed to call out to me. I couldn't stop myself. I flew down and the moment my hooves hit the ground, my wings disappeared. I didn't mind. I fell in love with Hoofishbofin immediately after I landed. The ponies were so welcoming and there was plenty to eat. I joined a band and now, all these years later, I've formed my own band."

Connie paused to wipe a tear from her eye. "Here's the thing. I had terrible luck but then it suddenly got much better. You can't steal someone else's luck, but you can help your own along. If you work hard and believe in yourself, then the good luck will eventually find you."

As Connie fell silent, Captain Rascal clapped and everyone joined in. Pippa clapped the loudest. She felt like she was about to burst.

"That girl was my aunt," she said breathlessly. "Aunt Maeve told me exactly the same story. As a girl she followed a rainbow until it led to you. She was so upset at how uncared for you were that she swapped you for her necklace. She needed a rope to lead you home and went to get one, but when she returned you were gone. No one believed her story. Her parents thought she'd made it up."

"Really!" Connie snorted, her brown eyes widening. "She never sent the flying horse then! Oh my goodness, the poor girl. She must have felt so unlucky."

"She didn't! Whenever Aunt Maeve feels unlucky now, she remembers how hungry and lonely you were and it reminds her that things aren't so bad after all."

"Your aunt's a special person. I would love to meet her again to say thank you." Connie sniffed. "You can take our pot of gold if you must, but promise me that you won't give it to Divine. The gold won't change your luck. Only you, the ponies of Chevalia, can do that!"

Captain Rascal picked a gold coin out of the pot and slipped it in his pocket. "Something to remember Captain Scallywag by." He gave Connie a cheeky grin. "You keep the pot. I doubt the gold will bring Divine happiness. Shiver me timbers, pirates. All aboard *The Jolly Horseshoe* for a lucky journey to mainland Chevalia."

The pirates cheered but Stardust still looked worried. Behind a hoof, she whispered to Pippa, "I'd feel much happier if we could find the unlucky horseshoe. What if the bad magic stops us from finding any luck ever again?"

"It won't," said Pippa bravely. She crossed her fingers and hoped that she was right.

Chapter 6

"The Happy Hooves and I have never visited the mainland," said Connie wistfully. "Will you take us?"

"For the price of a song," squawked the parrot, who was riding on Captain Rascal's shoulder.

Captain Rascal laughed. "Aye, for the price of a song, we will."

"It's a deal," cried Connie.

The pirate ponies lent a hoof to

get Rowan's harp aboard *The Jolly Horseshoe*.

"Careful," said Rowan as she edged her way across the hoof plank.

Pippa and Stardust came last. Pippa carried Connie's bodhran and her fingers itched to play it.

Connie must have noticed. Once on

board, she showed Pippa how to tap out a beat.

"You're a natural," she declared as Pippa beat out a rhythm to the tune of "My Pony Lies Over the Ocean."

"You play and I'll sing," Connie said.

"Can I?" Pippa was delighted. "It's truly my lucky day!" she declared.

"I feel lucky too," said Stardust in surprise as Rowan asked if she wanted to help with strumming the harp. "This is such fun."

"There's a good wind blowing," said Captain Rascal as the pirates cast off the mooring ropes. "With luck, we'll reach the mainland in no time."

Connie and the Happy Hooves played their instruments and sang the whole time *The Jolly Horseshoe* was at sea. They continued to sing as they came ashore on the beach near the Wild Forest.

The Wild Forest ponies came to the edge of the trees to see what all the noise was about. As Captain Rascal led everyone into the forest, the ponies shyly joined the musical parade. They hadn't gone far before the Wild Ponies forgot about being shy and joined in, singing with the Happy Hooves and the pirates at the tops of their voices.

Pippa was enjoying herself so much that she was surprised when they broke through the trees on the edge of the forest. Without stopping, Captain Rascal turned right and led the parade along the Fields to Mane Street.

"Look!" cried Stardust excitedly. "Everyone's lining the street to watch."

The ponies' glum faces and hunched shoulders disappeared. As the Happy Hooves and their new piratical backing band, The Jolly Horseshoes, sang and danced along Mane Street, the

watching ponies sang loudly and tapped their hooves in time.

"This is such fun," said Stardust as Captain Rascal took the parade in a circle around Canter's, Chevalia's prep school. "Look, Pippa, the pupils are bringing out instruments to join us. Pippa? Where are you going?"

A flash of silver in the sunlight had caught Pippa's eye. At first, she ignored it, but when it flashed again, she stopped in surprise. "I don't believe it!" Pippa strode purposefully toward a castle-shaped jungle gym in the school yard. "Of all the mean tricks!"

"Pippa?" Stardust went after her. "What's wrong?"

"Up there," Pippa said, and then

pointed to the tallest tower on the jungle gym.

Stardust gasped. "That is mean!"

The jungle gym was a replica of Stableside Castle, complete with eight tall towers, each with a different colored flag pictured with a golden horseshoe. All except for the smallest tower. Instead of a pink flag and golden horseshoe, identifying it as Princess Stardust's bedroom, someone had replaced the flag with a dark green, moldy-looking horseshoe.

"Divine," whispered Stardust, the color draining from her face. "Why did she pick my tower? Will I get all the bad luck?"

"No!" Pippa began to climb up the castle. "Remember what Connie told us. You can't steal someone else's luck. It's still a mean trick, though, leaving a bad spell in the foals' playground."

Pippa was so cross she didn't remember how much she disliked heights until she reached the top of the jungle gym. As she reached out to remove the unlucky horseshoe, she caught sight of Stardust, watching from the ground. Pippa's stomach dived to her feet, making her legs feel wobbly. She looked up quickly, fixing her eyes on the unlucky horseshoe perched on top of the tower, and she took a long breath in and out. There! That felt much better. Pippa grabbed the horseshoe. Its coldness made her shiver as she tucked it into the pocket of her jeans. The

horseshoe pressed against her leg, the bad magic buzzing faintly.

"Hooray!" cried Stardust, as Pippa slowly climbed down.

Pippa was in such a hurry to get back to the ground that she grew careless and slipped. Her hand shot out for a bar, but she missed.

"Help!"

Pippa gritted her teeth, bracing herself as the ground came nearer, but to her surprise she landed on something soft. "Stardust," Pippa said with surprise.

"I caught you!" Stardust was breathless with relief. "That was lucky! Divine's spell can't be working properly!"

"Thanks," said Pippa. "Quick, take

me out of the school yard. There's something I need to do, but not here."

Mystified, Stardust carried Pippa through the school gate.

"Take me to the cliffs," said Pippa, pointing to the Savannah, to the east of Mane Street.

Stardust galloped and Pippa held on tight. When they arrived at the edge of the island, Pippa slid from Stardust's back. She pulled the horseshoe out of her pocket and, with trembling fingers, held it upside down over the cliff face below.

After a few seconds Pippa heard a hiss like steam from a kettle when it starts to boil. She gripped the horse-shoe more tightly. With a *whoosh*, the

green magic spurted from the ends of the horseshoe and blew away in the wind, leaving a faint green trail.

"All gone!" said Pippa. She smiled as the air cleared. "The bad luck, it's drained out. This is just a regular horse-shoe now."

Stardust touched it with a hoof. "No

magic left at all," she agreed. "Clever Pippa. How did you know to do that?"

"Where I live, people hang horseshoes in their houses to bring them luck. I asked my riding teacher if I could have a horseshoe for my bedroom, and she warned me to hang it the right way up or the luck would run out. Come on," she added. "Let's rejoin the parade with this horseshoe and show everyone how lucky it is now!"

Chapter 7

Pippa and Stardust didn't reach Stable-side Castle. They barely made it to the end of Mane Street when they were met by a parade of Royal Ponies, led by Queen Moonshine and King Firestar, coming the other way.

Pippa dropped into a low curtsy with Stardust beside her. "Your Majesties," they murmured.

"What is going on?" asked Queen

Moonshine. Her deep-brown eyes took in the Happy Hooves and the singing pirates.

"How come everyone sounds so happy when their luck has gone?" King Firestar added.

"But it hasn't," said Pippa. Quickly, she explained what Connie had said about luck and how you could make your own. Queen Moonshine listened carefully, nodding thoughtfully as Pippa spoke.

"What about Divine? What about the bad-luck spell she cast over Chevalia? It doesn't matter how hard we try, we'll never be lucky with that hanging over us," Princess Crystal said as she pushed her way to the front.

Behind her, the ponies of the Royal

Court murmured in agreement. Crystal blushed with pleasure. One day she would be Queen of Chevalia, and she took her royal duties very seriously.

"We found the horseshoe that Divine used the spell on. It's in here." Pippa pulled the unlucky horseshoe out of her pocket. It didn't feel cold anymore as she held it up for everyone to see.

"Pippa tipped it upside down and the spell ran out," explained Stardust.

"Pippa MacDonald, we are *so* lucky to know you," said Queen Moonshine. "You always bring good luck!"

Pippa's face turned red from her chin to the tips of her ears. "Thanks," she said, "but I didn't do it on my own. Everyone helped." Pippa pointed at

Stardust, the pirate ponies, and Connie and her band.

Queen Moonshine smiled. "What's the music for?"

"Because everyone's so happy," Pippa explained. Then she added, "But, back in my world, today is called St. Patrick's Day, after a famous saint. It's a lucky day. People even celebrate it with a parade, a bit like this one."

"Then we shall celebrate St. Patrick's lucky day too," said Queen Moonshine. "Not just today, but every year."

"Really?" Pippa couldn't stop smiling as the music started up again and the parade began to play along Mane Street with the Royal Ponies following behind. As they circled Canter's for the third time, Pippa saw a hooded pony, half hidden behind the school gate, tapping a hoof as the musicians passed by.

"Divine!" she said, nudging Stardust.

Stardust's chest swelled indignantly. "She's got some nerve."

"I can't help feeling a little bit sorry for her," said Pippa generously. "She acts like no one likes her."

"That's because they don't."

Pippa shook her head, gently disagreeing with her friend. "She doesn't give anyone the chance to like her. It's a bit like finding luck. You have to work hard at making friends."

"I suppose." Stardust nudged Pippa fondly with her nose. "I'm so glad we're best friends."

"Me too," Pippa said as she hugged Stardust back, and when she drew away, Divine had gone.

Much later, after an impromptu feast in the middle of Mane Street where Pippa dined on pizza and fizzy strawberry juice, prepared especially for her, Captain Rascal sought Pippa out.

"Time to go home, Pippa. Stardust can come along too for the ride, if she'd like to."

"Definitely," said Stardust.

Pippa sighed, but then she remembered how she was always welcome to visit Chevalia. "I'm the luckiest girl in the world," she said happily.

"And I'm the luckiest pony in Chevalia," Stardust whinnied.

"The adventure's not over yet," said Captain Rascal. "Connie would like to come with us. She feels she owes your aunt an explanation. If that's fine by you?"

Pippa turned to Connie, who was shyly standing by a bucket of honeyed bran. "It's not *fine*. It's fantastic," she said warmly.

"Why, thank you, Pippa," said Connie.

It took Pippa ages to say all her good-byes, but at last she was on the beach, waiting to board *The Jolly Horseshoe*.

"All aboard, me hearties," cried Captain Rascal. "Prepare to sail."

Rosella and Triton, Chevalia's magical giant seahorses, escorted *The Jolly Horseshoe* out to sea.

"'Bye, Pippa. Come back soon,"

cried Rosella, saying good-bye with a flick of her pink tail.

"You're always welcome here," Triton reminded Pippa.

Pippa and Stardust stayed on the deck, the salty wind blowing through Pippa's hair and Stardust's mane as *The Jolly Horseshoe* flew through the waves. In no time at all, Pippa spotted land.

Lights twinkled on the water but onshore nothing moved. Pippa smiled to herself. How many other people were lucky enough to see their city frozen in time?

Unseen, *The Jolly Horseshoe* sailed along the river until it reached the park near Pippa's house. All of the pirate ponies wanted to accompany Pippa home, but Captain Rascal put his hoof down.

"It'll be a big enough surprise for Aunt Maeve to meet one pony, let alone a whole pirate crew."

Three ponies went in the end: Captain Rascal, Connie, and Stardust. Captain Rascal threw tiny stones at the window of the living room, where Aunt Maeve was sleeping on the pull-out sofa. When she opened the window, the ponies hid in the shadows. Aunt Maeve rubbed her eyes and yawned as she looked outside. "Pippa, what are you doing out of bed?" she asked.

"I want to show you something," said Pippa.

"Can't it wait until the morning?"

"*Pleeease*, Aunt Maeve, it's really important."

It took a lot of persuading, but finally Aunt Maeve came out to the garden in her dressing gown and shoes.

Connie stepped out of her hiding place and Aunt Maeve stared at her in astonishment. "Where did you come from? You look like my childhood pony from Ireland."

"That's because she is your child-hood pony," said Pippa.

Aunt Maeve threw her arms around Connie. "I *knew* you were real. I'm so lucky to have found you."

"Shhh," said Pippa nervously. What would she say if Aunt Maeve woke everyone up!

But the family slept on while Aunt Maeve made a fuss over Connie, and Pippa persuaded her to ride Connie around the neighborhood. When they returned, Pippa sensed that Captain Rascal was getting restless.

"I have to take Connie back now," she said.

Aunt Maeve slid from Connie's back and wrapped her arms around her neck. "I'm dreaming," she said and shook her dark head. "I know I'm still asleep, but this is the nicest dream ever."

"You're not," said Pippa, smiling at her aunt. "But it is time to go back to bed."

Aunt Maeve sighed deeply. "Thanks,

Pippa. You always make me feel so lucky to have you as family."

"Me too," said Pippa, pushing her aunt indoors. "I'm just *so* lucky to have you as my aunt."

With Aunt Maeve back inside, Captain Rascal and Stardust came out of hiding.

"'Bye, Stardust," said Pippa as they hugged. "I'll miss you."

"'Bye, Pippa. See you soon, my lucky friend."

Together, Stardust, Connie, and Captain Rascal left for the park. Pippa waved until they turned a corner and disappeared.

She felt like the luckiest girl in the whole world.

JOURNEY BACK TO THE VERY BEGINNING
OF PIPPA AND THE PONIES' ADVENTURES
IN THE WONDROUS LAND OF CHEVALIA . . .

SOMEONE HAS STOLEN THE HORSESHOES
THAT GIVE CHEVALIA ITS MAGIC! CAN
PIPPA AND PRINCESS STARDUST WORK
TOGETHER TO FIND THEM?

Turn the page to read a sneak peek . . .

Pippa MacDonald turned her pony, Snowdrop, toward the last jump, a solid-looking red-and-white wall. Snowdrop pricked up her ears. She snorted with excitement and sped up.

"Steady, girl," Pippa said, pulling gently on the reins.

None of the other riders had jumped a clean round. Pippa and Snowdrop were the last to go, and if they cleared the wall they would win the competition, taking home a silver cup and a blue ribbon. As the wall came closer, Pippa forced back the nervous, fluttery feeling growing in her stomach.

"We can do this," she whispered to Snowdrop.

She leaned forward, standing up in her stirrups, loosening the reins as she pushed her pony to the jump. Snowdrop leaped over it eagerly, carrying Pippa upward. For a magical moment it felt like they were flying. Any fear of heights simply slipped away. Fresh air rushed at Pippa's face, lifting her dark, wavy hair that was neatly held in place by a hairnet. Snowdrop cleared the wall, happily flicking her tail as she landed.

"Yes!" Pippa shouted, galloping Snowdrop over the finish line.

The crowd cheered and screamed, but one voice shouted louder than the rest.

"Pippa! Are you awake? It's time to go."

Pippa jolted out of her dream, nearly falling off her bed as Snowdrop, the show jumping arena, and the cheering crowds vanished. She blinked and stared around the small bedroom she shared with her big sister, Miranda.

It was easy to see which side of the room was Pippa's. Her wall was totally covered with pictures of ponies—big ones, small ones, black, brown, chestnut, roan, palomino, gray. Pippa's favorite picture of all was of Snowdrop, a silver-colored pony with deep-brown eyes.

Miranda's side used to have horse pictures too, but it was now covered with posters of boys—some were famous movie stars but most were in bands. Both sisters thought the other one's decorations were silly.

"Are you ready, sweetheart?" Mom asked from the doorway.

"Almost!" Pippa called, jumping off the bed and following her mom downstairs. "Did you remember to pack my bathing suit?"

"Of course," Mom said, smiling. "Now go get ready!"

☆

It was boiling hot and Pippa was glad that she, her mom, Miranda, and their little brother, Jack, were going on vacation, trading their apartment in the city for a cottage by the sea. Pippa was so excited she trotted up and down the pavement, riding an imaginary pony as she waited for Mom to unlock the car so that they could load the luggage into the trunk.

"You're so immature," Miranda said, rolling her eyes as she climbed into the front seat.

Mom snapped Jack into his car seat and Pippa took her usual seat in the back, beside her brother.

"We're off!" cheered Pippa as Mom started the engine.

Dreamily, Pippa stared out the window, watching the busy city streets change to green fields filled with horses, cows, and sheep, until at last they arrived at their vacation home.

"Wow! Is it all ours?" Pippa exclaimed, as Mom pulled up in front of a small, white cottage surrounded by a huge yard. "I could have a pony if we lived here."

"Yes, the yard's big enough!" Mom

agreed, digging in her handbag for the key to the front door.

The cottage was right by the water. Pippa breathed deeply, loving the smell of the fresh, salty air.

"Can we go to the beach?" she asked.

Mom laughed at her impatience. "Let's unpack the car first. If we're going to the beach, you'll want to take your buckets and shovels."

"I'll help," Pippa said, pulling her bag from the trunk.

The cottage was even prettier inside. Pippa loved the attic bedroom, even though she had to share it with Miranda. It had sloping walls and a sea view, and, to Pippa's delight, there was an old horseshoe nailed to one of the roof beams.

"Horseshoes are lucky," she said happily.

Pippa skipped down the stairs into the kitchen, where Mom was searching their luggage for the bag of food.

"We'll have our lunch on the beach," she said, packing sandwiches, cupcakes, apples, and drinks into a picnic basket.

☆

The gate at the back of the yard opened onto a winding path that led down to the sea. Pippa was too excited to walk. Instead she galloped down the path, pretending to be a wild stallion, until she reached a horseshoe-shaped cove. Pippa stared in wonder at the golden sand and sparkling blue water stretching away from her.

The cove felt so secret and special it made Pippa's insides buzz with excitement.

"It's magic," she whispered softly.

Pulling off her sandals, she ran across the powdery sand to the sea, where tiny, white-crested waves were licking the shore. Just as Pippa was about to paddle in the water, she saw something far away. What was that at the mouth of the cove?

Pippa stared in amazement at two animals splashing in the water. "They look just like seahorses!" she gasped.

Pippa raised her arm to shield her eyes from the sun so she could take a better look. They really did look like seahorses, and they were almost as big as real horses, with gracefully curved necks bobbing above the water and long spines sticking up along spiky manes. One horse was pale pink and the other was green with dark freckles. Pippa blinked and rubbed her eyes. Was she imagining things? When she looked again the two animals were still there, splashing water at each other with their curled tails.

Behind her Pippa could hear Mom, Miranda, and Jack laughing together as they made their way to the beach.

"Quick!" she called, waving at them. "Look at this!"

"What is it, sweetheart?"

"Seahorses," Pippa said.

"Where? I can't see them!" Jack cried.

"Seahorses!" Miranda exclaimed.

"How can you see a tiny seahorse from here?"

"They're giant ones," Pippa said.

"I can't see anything." Mom stared out at the sea.

Miranda giggled as she ran over. "I see them! The red one's wearing a hat!"

Pippa's heart leaped, then sank right down to her bare toes. Miranda was teasing her! Besides, the sea was empty now. The seahorses had disappeared.

"I did see two seahorses," Pippa insisted. "They were playing together."

"Don't be silly, Pip. There's no such thing as a giant seahorse," Miranda said meanly.

"Pippa, you're too big for that sort of

make-believe," Mom said gently. "Come and help me set out the picnic."

Pippa gazed at the sea, but there was nothing there except for the sea-gulls gliding over the bay. But the seahorses *were* real—Pippa knew she hadn't imagined them. Confused, she hurried after Mom.

"Do I have to eat now?" she asked. "I want to go in the water first."

"Go ahead," Mom said. "Be careful. Don't go in deeper than your knees."

Pippa ran back to the water's edge. The sea was lovely and warm. She waded out until she was knee deep. The water was so clear she could still see her feet. Pippa wiggled her toes in the sand.

"Ooooh," she said. "That tickles!"

Two tiny seahorses were swimming around her feet.

"Wow! This place is full of seahorses!"

Pippa bent down for a closer look.

The moment her fingers touched the water they began to tingle. The feeling was so incredible that Pippa felt sure it was some kind of magic. Gently, she moved her fingers to get one of the seahorses to swim to her hand. The tiny animal was almost there when, suddenly, with a loud *whoosh*, the water rose up in the shape of the head and front legs of a galloping horse.

"Eek!" Pippa squealed.

Two giant seahorses popped through

the water and examined Pippa with their big eyes.

"You *are* real!" she exclaimed. "I knew I hadn't imagined it."

Pippa waded closer to the giant creatures and gently stroked their noses.

"Your name, Pippa, is short for Philippa, which means *lover of ponies*," said the pink seahorse.

"That's right," said Pippa, who couldn't believe she was talking to a giant seahorse.

"Then you are the one," said the green seahorse.

"My name is Rosella," the pink seahorse continued. "And this is Triton. We've come to take you to a place that needs your help."